PENGUIN DREAMS

dedicated to
all of
THE BABIES.

PENGUIN DREAMS

J. otto Seibold and V. L. Walsh

SCHOLASTIC INC.

New York Toronto London Auckland Sydney
Mexico City New Delhi Hong Kong

Shhhhhh...

Chongo Chingi is

SLEEPING

**But even when
sleeping,
a penguin keeps
thinking.**

Chongo Chingi is

DREAMING

Thoughts are flying
round and round,
thoughts of flying
off the ground.

"Icicle-barnicle,
what shall we do?"

"We'll meet in the water!"
and off they flew.

One to the water,
one to the air...

Chongo didn't know he could go up there.

honk-honk

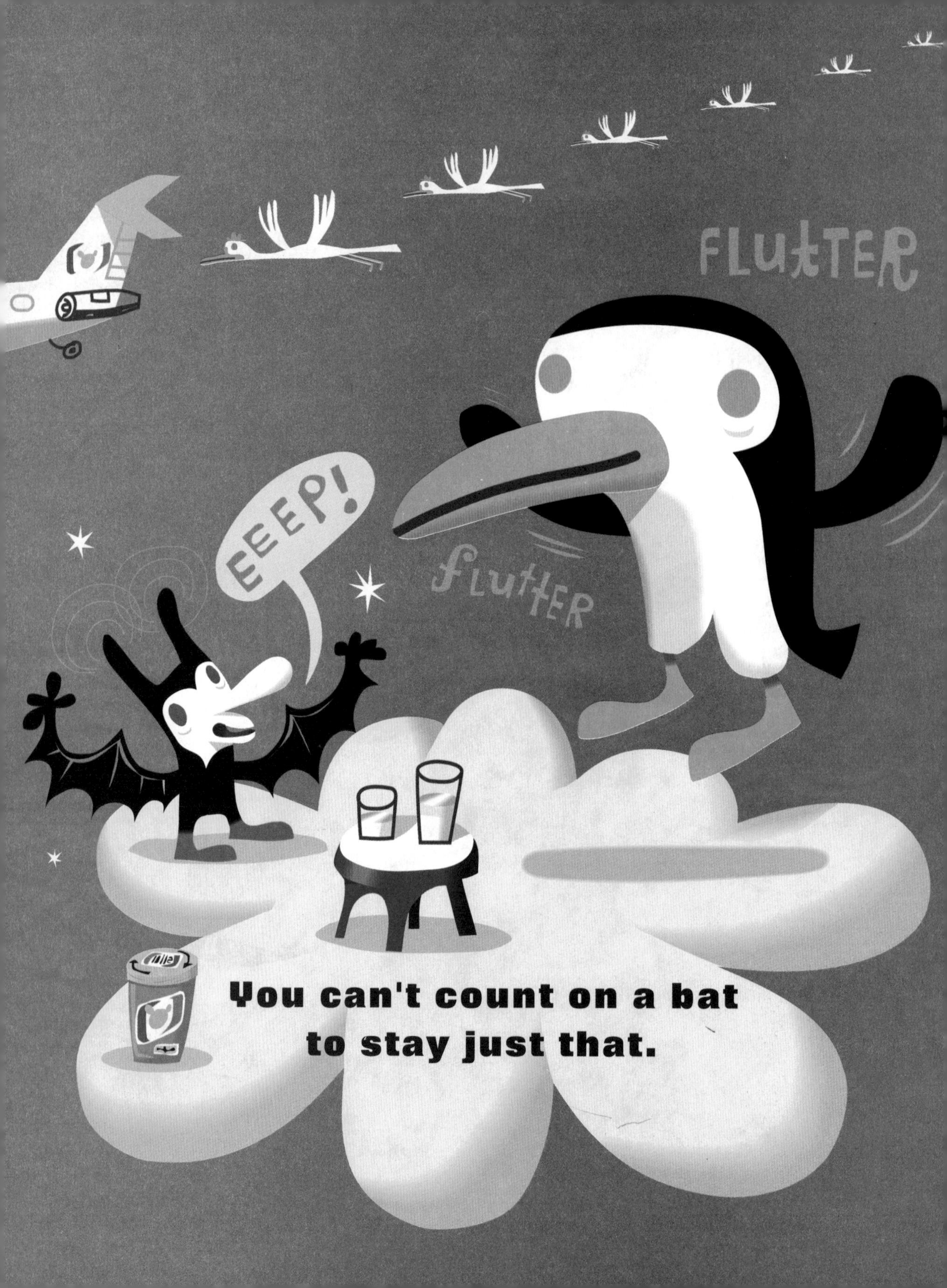

You can't count on a bat to stay just that.

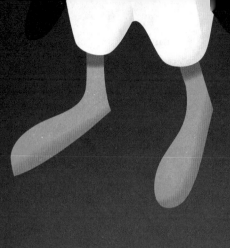

KERSPLOOEY

HELLO

GHOUD BYE

Space is no trouble...

...if you float like a bubble.

**Ring-aling-ling...
Ding-dong-dingi...
Time to wake-up
Chongo Chingi!**

ISBN 0-439-21736-9

12 11 10 9 8 7 6 5 4   1 2 3 4 5/0

Printed in the U.S.A.   23

First Scholastic printing, December 2000

Book design by J. Otto Siebold.
Typeset in Honky and Rosewood.
The illustrations in this book were rendered on an Apple computer Power Macintosh 8500/120. Using Adobe Illustrator v6.0 software.

beak

belly

eyes

flippers

boots

THE QUOTE THAT APPEARS ON THE BACK
COVER IS BY THEADORA WALSH

AGE 3
1995

orange

white

blue

black

tangerine